HOW TO TELL IF IT IS A HIPPOPOTAMUS
HEFTYTHUMP
BUMBLEBUFFER
NOTE: NOT TO BE MISTAKEN FOR AN ELEPHANT'S TRUNDLEBUMPER
GRUBTUB
FLOBBLEWAFFLER
PLODDERS
MAR 2017

That's NOT a HIPPOPOTAMUS!

Written by **Juliette MacIver**

Illustrated by **Sarah Davis**

GECKO PRESS

At Don's Safari, understand,
we've every creature in the land.
All roaming wild, safe and free.
So many beasts for you to see!

That's a lie! A whopper, Miss!
He's got no hippopotamus!

Of course I have! Come right this way!
He's by this lakeside every day.

SEE THE AMAZING HIPPOPOTAMUS

Oh my giddy gad, **he's gone!**

We'll find him! Don't you worry, Don!
We'll spread out wide. Hunt high and low.
We'll have him back before you know!

Golly, Miss! A lot amiss.
A missing hippopotamus!
Good thing we're here. The best, hands down,
of hippo-hunters in the town.

I see him, Miss! He's super tall!

I'll fetch him in no time at all.

I got 'im, Miss!
I got 'im, Miss!
I KNEW that I could spot 'im, Miss!

That's NOT a hippopotamus!

We'll do it good and proper, Miss!
We'll find that hippopotamus.
Good thing we're here. The most superior
hippo-hunters in the area.

I see him, Miss! He's on the ground.
I'll get him while he's snuffling round.

I got 'im, Miss!
I got 'im, Miss!
I got 'im by his trotter, Miss!

That's NOT a hippopotamus!

A missing hippopotamus!
Need a hippo-spotter, Miss?
Good thing we're here. The greatest band
of hippo-hunters in the land.

I see him, Miss! He's very quick!
I'll chase him with my pointy stick!

I got 'im, Miss!
I got 'im, Miss!
I KNEW that I could stop 'im, Miss!

That's NOT a hippopotamus!

A missing hippopotamus!
The trail is getting hotter, Miss!
Good thing we're here. The very best
of hippo-hunters in the west.

I see him, Miss! I'm on his trail.
I'll grab him by his stripy tail!

I got 'im, Miss!
I got 'im, Miss!
He smells all stinky rotten, Miss!

Lilah's quite a plotter, Miss.
She'll find that hippopotamus!
Good thing we're here. For all it's worth:
best hippo-hunters on the Earth.

I see him, Miss! I see his fin!
Watch me, Miss. I'm diving in!

I got 'im, Miss!
I got 'im, Miss!
He's slippery like an otter, Miss!

That's NOT a hippopotamus!

Stinking hippopotamus!
What a lot of bother, Miss.
He's ridiculed the lot of us.
We're nothing but the most forlorn
of hippo-hunters ever born.

Home we go, then. Fingers crossed
that blooming hippo isn't lost.

We got 'im, Miss!
We got 'im, Miss!
We got 'im by his bottom, Miss!

So THAT'S a hippopotamus!

This edition first published in 2016 by Gecko Press
PO Box 9335, Marion Square, Wellington 6141, New Zealand
info@geckopress.com

Reprinted 2016

Text © Juliette MacIver 2016
Illustrations © Sarah Davis 2016

Distributed in the United States and Canada by Lerner Publishing Group, www.lernerbooks.com
Distributed in the UK by Bounce Sales & Marketing, www.bouncemarketing.co.uk
Distributed in Australia by Scholastic Australia, www.scholastic.com.au
Distributed in New Zealand by Upstart Distribution, www.upstartpress.co.

Designed by Vida & Luke Kelly, New Zealand
Printed in China by Everbest Printing Co. Ltd, an accredited ISO 14001 & FSC certified printer

ISBN hardback: 978-1-927271-96-4
ISBN paperback: 978-1-927271-97-1
Ebook available

For more curiously good books, visit www.geckopress.com